My Little Golden Book
About
GOD

By Jane Werner Watson
Illustrated by Eloise Wilkin

A GOLDEN BOOK • NEW YORK

Copyright © 1956, renewed 1984 by Random House, Inc. All rights reserved. Published in the United States by Golden Books, an imprint of Random House Children's Books, a division of Random House, Inc., New York. Originally published in 1956 by Simon and Schuster, Inc., and Artists and Writers Guild, Inc. GOLDEN BOOKS, A GOLDEN BOOK, A LITTLE GOLDEN BOOK, the G colophon, and the distinctive gold spine are registered trademarks of Random House, Inc. A Little Golden Book Classic is a trademark of Random House, Inc.
www.goldenbooks.com
www.randomhouse.com/kids
Educators and librarians, for a variety of teaching tools, visit us at
www.randomhouse.com/teachers
Library of Congress Control Number: 2007922406
ISBN: 978-0-307-02105-2
Printed in the United States of America
27 26 25 24 23 22 21 20

GOD IS GREAT.

Look at the stars in the evening sky,
so many millions of miles away
that the light you see shining left its star
long, long years before you were born.

Yet even beyond the farthest star,
God knows the way.
Think of the snow-capped mountain peaks.
Those peaks were crumbling away with
age before the first people lived on earth.
Yet when they were raised up sharp and new
God was there, too.

Bend down to touch the smallest flower.
Watch the busy ant tugging at his load.
See the flash of jewels on the insect's back.
This tiny world your two hands could span,
like the oceans and mountains and far-off stars,
God planned.

Think of our earth, spinning in space

so that now, for a day of play and work
we face the sunlight, then we turn away—

to the still, soft darkness for rest and sleep.
This, too, is God's doing.

For GOD IS GOOD.

God gives us everything we need—
shelter from cold and wind and rain,
clothes to wear and food to eat.

God gives us flowers, the songs of birds,
the laughter of brooks, the deep song of the sea.

He sends the sunshine

to make things grow,

sends in its turn
the needed rain.

God makes us grow, too, with minds and eyes
to look about our wonderful world,
to see its beauty, to feel its might.

He gives us a small, still voice in our hearts
to help us tell wrong from right.
God gives us hopes and wishes and dreams,
plans for our grown-up years ahead.

He gives us memories of yesterdays,
so that happy times and people we love
we can keep with us always in our hearts.
For GOD IS LOVE.

God is the love of our mother's kiss,

the warm, strong hug of our daddy's arms.

God is in all the love we feel
for playmates and family and friends.

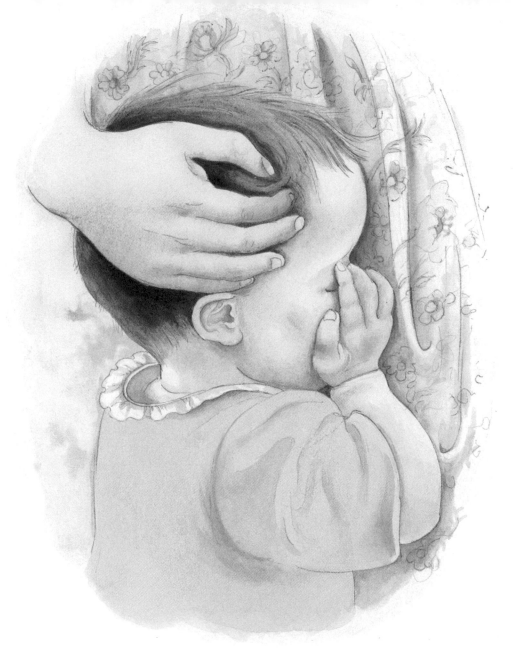

When we're hurt or sorry or lonely or sad,
if we think of God, He is with us there.

God whispers to us in our hearts:
"Do not fear, I am here,
And I love you, my dear.
Close your eyes and sleep tight,
For tomorrow will be bright.
All is well, dear child.
Good night."